If i could keep you little...

WRITTEN AND ILLUSTRATED BY
Marianne Richmond

sourcebooks
jabberwocky

Text and illustrations copyright © 2010 Marianne Richmond
Cover and internal design © 2010 by Sourcebooks, Inc.

Published by Sourcebooks Jabberwocky, an imprint of Sourcebooks, Inc.
P.O. Box 4410, Naperville, Illinois 60567-4410
(630) 961-3900
Fax: (630) 961-2168
www.jabberwockykids.com

Library of Congress Cataloging-in-Publication data is on file with the publisher.

Source of Production: Leo Paper Group, Heshan City, Guandong Province, China
Date of Production: August 2011
Run Number: 15961

Printed and bound in China.
LEO 10 9 8 7 6 5

Dedicated to my C, A, J, and W.
I adored you little. And I am in awe
of who you are becoming.
—MR

If I could keep
you little,

I'd **hum** you

lullabies.

But then I'd miss you *singing*

your concert's *big* surprise.

If I could keep you little,

I'd **hold** your hand
everywhere.

But then I'd miss you **knowing,**

"I can go...

you stay there.**"**

If I could keep you little,

I'd **kiss** your
cuts and **scrapes.**

But then I'd miss you *learning* from **your own mistakes.**

If I could
keep you little,

I'd **strap**
you in
real
tight.

But then I'd miss
you *swinging*
from your
treetop height.

If I could
keep you little,

I'd decide on
matching
clothes.

But then I'd miss you **choosing**

dots on top
and **stripes below.**

If I could keep you little,

I'd cut your bread into shapes.

But then I'd miss you **finding,**

"Hey! I *like* ketchup
with my grapes!"

If I could keep
you little,

I'd tell you **stories**
every night.

But then I'd miss
you *reading*
the words
you've learned
by sight.

If I could keep you little,

I'd push you
anywhere.

But then I'd miss you **feeling**

your speed
from *here to there!*

If I could keep you little,
I'd pick for you **a friend** or two.

But then I'd miss you **finding** friends you like *who like you, too!*

If I could keep you little,

we'd **finger-paint** our art.

But then I'd miss you **creating**

stories from

your *heart*.

If I could
   keep you little,

I'd push
   your *ducky* float.

But then I'd miss
you *feeling*
the **wind** behind
summer's
boat.

If I could keep you little,

we'd *nap* in our **fort** midday.

But then I'd miss you **sharing**

adventures from camp **away.**

If I could keep you little, I'd *fly* you *with my* feet.

But then I'd miss you **seeing** **sky and clouds** from your seat.

If I could
keep you little,

I'd keep you
close to me.

But then I'd miss you **growing** into *who you're meant to be!*

Beloved author and illustrator Marianne Richmond has touched the lives of millions for nearly two decades through her award-winning books, greeting cards, and other gift products that offer people the most heartfelt way to connect.

If I Could Keep You Little is inspired from watching her four kids grow while wistfully recalling memories of a "littler" time. "The cover image captures the flying game I used to play with them," says Marianne. "Believe it or not, they were truly afraid to let go of my hands for fear of falling onto the carpet!" she laughs. Now she is forever amazed by their growing independence—from one's natural golf swing to another's ability to tell compelling, made-up stories to her stuffed animal students.

As for the author herself, she wrinkles her nose at the thought of ketchup on grapes. But jelly on eggs? "The perfect Sunday breakfast," she laughs.

Also available from author & illustrator Marianne Richmond:

978-0-9753-5288-5	978-1-9340-8226-3	978-0-9741-4653-9	978-1-9340-8225-6
$15.95 U.S.	$15.95 U.S.	$15.95 U.S.	$15.95 U.S.
$18.99 CAN	$18.99 CAN	$18.99 CAN	$18.95 CAN
£10.99 UK	£10.99 UK	£10.99 UK	£10.99 UK